SEASIDE

Serenade

A Seaside Summers Short Story
Love in Bloom Series

Melissa Foster

ISBN-13: 978-1948868396

Cover Design: Elizabeth Mackey

A Note to Readers

Friendships and family abound during this fun-filled weekend of love, laughter, and happily ever afters! Spend the evening catching up with our Seaside friends in this Valentine's Day celebration and fall in love with our newest Seaside couple, Brock and Cree!

I have wanted to write Brock Garner's story since the day I first met him, years ago, and I am thrilled to have finally fit it into my writing schedule. Seaside Serenade is a great way to get to know some of our Seaside Summers friends, and then you can go back and read each of their love stories. **If this is your first introduction to Seaside Summers**, please note that this is a *flirt*, a short story spanning one weekend. As with all my stories, you will get a sexy, fun, romantic story with a wonderful happily ever after, and never any cliffhangers. Like all Love in Bloom books, flirts are written to stand alone, so jump right in and enjoy the fun, sexy, and emotional ride.

The best way to keep up to date with new releases, sales, and exclusive content is to sign up for my newsletter. www.MelissaFoster.com/Newsletter

If this is your first Love in Bloom story, then you have a whole series of loyal, sexy, and wickedly naughty heroes and smart, sassy heroines to catch up with. The characters from each family series within the Love in Bloom world cross into other family series and make appearances in future books so you never miss an engagement, wedding, or birth.

Start reading the Love in Bloom big-family romance collection FREE with the series starters that kicked-off the sensation. www.Melissafoster.com/LIBFree

A Love in Bloom series checklist, and family trees are available for download on the Reader Goodies page on my website: www.MelissaFoster.com/RG

Be sure to check out my online bookstore for pre-orders, early releases, bundles, and exclusive discounts on ebooks, print, and audiobooks. Ebooks can be sent to the e-reader of your choice and audiobooks can be listened to on the free and easy-to-use BookFunnel app. Shop my store: shop.melissafoster.com

Happy reading!
Melissa

CHAPTER ONE

WHOEVER SAID WORKING out was a good substitute for sex had never been around Cree Redmond, a petite raven-haired beauty who preferred combat boots to sneakers. Brock Garner was a local boxing champ, and he was a big dude at six foot four and two hundred and thirty pounds, but that perky little sexpot could take him to his knees with one innocent smile. He stole a glance at her as he danced around the boxing ring with his buddy Sawyer Bass, another boxer-turned-trainer. Cree was leaning over the counter with a pencil in her mouth, studying the trainers' schedules, moving her fine ass to the beat of whatever music she had on at the front desk, completely fucking oblivious to the hard-ons she gave Brock every damn—

Umph! Sawyer's glove connected with Brock's jaw, snapping him from his Cree trance. Brock narrowed his eyes, focusing on his opponent, who was grinning around his mouthpiece.

Asshole.

Sawyer had taken a cheap shot, but it was Brock's own fault. Nothing had ever broken his focus when he was boxing until Cree had come into his club looking for a job four months ago. He'd never forget the first time he'd seen her. She'd been helping to entertain the children of the guests at Sky and Sawyer's quadruple wedding, during which Brock's sister Jana had also gotten married. He'd been awestruck by her innocent brown eyes and sunny disposition, a glaring contrast to her head-to-toe black clothing, the colorful tattoos running down her arm and snaking up her neck, and the black Harley on which she'd arrived. But then he'd seen her around town with Justin Wicked, a rough-looking, bearded biker. Justin and his brother owned Cape Stone, a stone distribution and stonemasonry company. They were both stand-up guys, and after realizing Justin and Cree were dating, Brock had firmly placed her in the not-available category. Hiring her was the best and worst decision of his life. Clients loved her vivacious personality as much as he did, but seeing her prance around in tight yoga pants and barely there tank tops was pure torture. And ever since she'd started taking dance classes from his sister Jana, Cree had been practicing and shaking her fantastic booty on the job, making it hard for him to think of anything else.

Well, other than having her naked in my arms…

Brock lowered his chin, studying Sawyer's movements. Sawyer had been concussed one too many times, and he no longer competed professionally, but Brock didn't go easy on him. Not that Sawyer wanted him to; the guy was tough as nails. Brock saw an opening and took it, connecting with Sawyer's ribs and then landing an uppercut to his jaw, while skillfully avoiding Sawyer's retaliations.

Sawyer's phone alarm went off, indicating the end of their practice. Brock's eyes shifted to Cree as he stripped off his gloves and took out his mouthpiece.

"Nice fight," Sawyer said sarcastically. "Maybe they can open a *pansy* division for you."

Brock scoffed as he climbed out of the ring. "If that were a real fight, I'd have won."

"If that were a real fight, I would have actually fought."

The bell over the door sounded, and Sky breezed in, her long colorful skirt whipping around her boots. She waved to Sawyer, then stopped to chat with Cree. Sky's brother Hunter was married to Brock's sister Jana. They were all pretty tight.

"Be right there, babe," Sawyer called out as he stuffed

his equipment in his bag.

Sky owned a tattoo shop in Provincetown, which, like most towns on the Outer Cape, was all but closed down for the winter. Cree worked for Sky in the summer, along with holding down a handful of other part-time jobs. As the oldest of four, raised by strict parents who believed in traditional values, Brock was a planner. He'd known he wanted to own a boxing club since he was a teenager. Going from job to job as Cree—and Brock's sister Jana used to—would drive him batty. But that wasn't why he'd hired Cree full-time at the club when he only needed a part-time employee for the winter. Giving her job stability probably should have been the reason, but his decision had been solely based on wanting to be around her. She was the happiest, friendliest, most beautiful person inside and out, and he'd jumped at the chance to have her in his life any way he could.

"You should bring Cree to the Valentine's Day party tomorrow at Undercover. I bet she'd dig hearing the *Beast* sing," Sawyer said, referring to the name Brock used when he fought competitively.

He and Sawyer sang in an a capella group called A Capella Boys along with Sawyer's former boxing coach, Roach Regan, who also trained other fighters at the club. Their group had started as a joke, but they had too much fun to give it up. Now they occasionally sang at open-mic nights at Undercover, Brock's brother Colton's bar.

Sawyer smirked and said, "Although I wouldn't suggest having Little Miss Distraction watch you compete. You could lose your undefeated title."

Brock glowered at him. Then he looked across the gym at Cree, catching her gazing at him while she talked to Sky. Her cheeks pinked up, and she quickly shifted her eyes away, as she often did, but she'd already lit the wick between them, and his body heated up. Sometimes the things she said felt a hell of a lot like she was flirting, but then Justin would drive her to or from work, reminding him that she was firmly off-limits, and he'd realized it had only been in his head.

"She probably already has plans."

"She's still hanging out with Justin? She must really love his…*motorcycle*." Sawyer pulled on his coat and swung his bag over his shoulder with a smart-ass look in his eyes.

Brock gritted his teeth. "He drives a truck during the winter."

In addition to her motorcycle, Cree owned a bright yellow Toyota Tercel, which had been the first clue as to how serious she and Justin were. It wasn't like she couldn't drive herself to work. If she were *his*, he'd have her ditch that shitty car and he'd buy her a four-wheel-drive Land Rover so she didn't kill herself in the snow.

But she wasn't his, and in case he'd forgotten that annoying fact, the lack of either a Harley or a Tercel in the parking lot was a glaring reminder.

"If you were any other guy, I'd say to make your move," Sawyer said. "But it's not your style to hit on some other guy's woman. Sorry, man."

"Sometimes I wish I were an asshole." He glanced at Cree. She had her earbuds back in again and was bopping to the beat as Sky talked on her cell phone. "But if Wicked ever hurts her, you can guarantee I'll go ape shit on his ass."

"I hear ya. See you tomorrow night."

After Sawyer and Sky left, Cree pulled out her earbuds and said, "Hey, Brock? I've got twenty minutes. Would you mind giving me a few more pointers before I take off?"

A few weeks ago Cree had asked him to teach her to box. She said she wanted to learn to hit because a girl needed to know how to protect herself. With Justin around, Brock doubted she ever went anywhere alone or had to worry about that. But he believed wholeheartedly in self-defense, and it gave him a chance to get up close and personal with Cree, but damn, those black yoga pants did him in every time.

"Sure." *I don't mind taking another cold shower.*

"Yay! Thank you!" She came around the front desk with a bounce in her step as she whipped her T-shirt over her head, flashing an effervescent smile and revealing more of the colorful tattoos on her left arm and right shoulder. He tried like hell not to lower his eyes, but *damn*. The skintight crop-top/bra combo deal she wore left *nothing* to the imagination. Her nipples pressed against the thin material. His fingers curled against the urge to touch her. That should be enough to distract him from her bare stomach, but the glistening silver ring in her belly button made his mouth water.

"Ready, big guy?" She walked backward, moving her fists like she was fighting. "I'm feeling good tonight. I think I can nail the speed bag this time."

He'd like to nail her.

Great. That thought brought an instant hard-on.

Up close and personal took on a whole new level when she used the speed bag. At least she didn't want to focus on footwork tonight. He'd tried to get her to wear sneakers during their first lesson, but she'd insisted on wearing those clumsy combat boots. When they concentrated on footwork, she often tripped, landing in his arms. Lucretia "Cree" Redmond was the very definition of heaven and hell.

"And if we're quick," she said with a spark of excitement in her eyes, "maybe you can show me some fancy footwork."

There was no water cold enough to douse the flames that idea sent coursing through his veins.

"Spin it around, sweetheart," he said when they reached the speed bag. "Show me what you've got."

She faced the bag, wiggling her butt, hands fisted, and said, "I've got it this time. I don't even think I need to do the fingertip thing. Watch."

She stood with her feet a little too wide and lowered her elbows too much, but he bit his tongue because she was so freaking adorable and excited he didn't want to steal her joy. She inhaled deeply and thrust her breasts out. *Freaking torture.* Smile still in place, she nodded once and hit the bag. She even got a second hit in, but then it all went to hell. She hit the bag too hard, losing the rhythm, and her next two punches missed the bag altogether.

Her arms stretched down toward the floor, and she looked up at the ceiling with a loud groan. "I'm *such* a girl!"

"That's a good thing." He stepped closer, bringing his body flush with her back. He inhaled her sweet scent, the scent that invaded his darkest fantasies. The ones in which he stripped her bare and feasted on every inch of her.

Christ. He was a glutton for punishment. "What do I always tell you?"

She leaned back against him just enough to make his cock throb and said, "That fighting like a girl is a compliment."

"Right. There's no competition between girls and guys. Girls can be as tough as they want or need to be. But it starts with the correct stance." He guided her left hip back. "Your entire body should face the bag."

"I remember," she said a little breathily, standing straighter.

"And your hands are too low and wide. You want to keep them in tight. Tighter is always better." *Aw, fuck.* His mind went straight to the gutter.

"Like this?" She held her hands closer.

"Almost." He guided her hands into position. "It might be easier if we do it together. Put your hands over mine, and I'll show you the motion."

Her slender hands moved over his as he began hitting the bag with his fingertips. "Keeping your hands close to the bag will help you control each hit. Remember to use small, circular motions. Hit it twice with the left hand, twice with the right, until you get it down."

"Get it down. Got it."

He couldn't resist pushing the boundaries, because fuck, didn't he deserve it after all this? "Think of the bag as a new lover. Hit it too hard, and you may not be able to keep up. Too soft, and you'll both be left unsatisfied."

"Uh-huh," she said huskily.

"But when you find that perfect rhythm, you'll know it because you'll *never* want to stop."

Her fingers slipped between his, holding tighter as he tapped the bag. Her ass brushed over his cock, and he sure as hell never wanted to stop.

"You're really *good*," she said breathily. "I bet you never leave anyone unsatisfied." Her face whipped toward his. "*Anything!* Never leave *anything* unsatisfied. I want to do you. *It!* I want to do *it!* Hit the *bag!*" She pulled her hands back as if she'd been burned, her cheeks stained crimson. "*Ohmygod!* Fire me, *please.*"

She was so fucking cute and flustered, he couldn't stifle a laugh.

She covered her face with her hands and said, "*God.* Justin's right. I'm going to get myself in trouble working here."

Talk about a cold shower.

Shit. This was all his fault. He had no business toying with her. He gently lowered her hands and said, "It's my fault. It's been a long day, and that analogy came out of nowhere. It was probably inappropriate. I'm sorry."

"No. It was fine. It's *me.* It's always me." She grabbed her shirt and tugged it over her head as she stalked up front.

He followed her, feeling like an ass. "Cree, don't be silly. You're amazing."

"Amazingly *awkward.*" She shoved her earbuds in her ears and started navigating on her phone, cutting him off completely.

She gathered her things and shoved them in her messenger bag. She pushed her arm into her black leather coat and the earbuds came unplugged. Music blasted from the phone, and the most beautiful voice he'd ever heard filled the air. It was throaty and eclectic, like a mix of Janis Joplin and Stevie Nicks.

"*Who* is that?"

"No one." Her cheeks flamed and she dove for her phone, but he snagged it first and held it out of her reach as recognition hit him.

"Holy shit, Cree. That's *you*."

"Give it to me!" She jumped, trying to reach her phone, but at five two she didn't stand a chance.

"You can *sing*," he said with awe as her voice sailed from the phone.

"No, I can't." She jumped again. "Give it to me."

"Not a chance, sweetheart. You're really talented. What song is that?" He didn't recognize the lyrics, which were dark and light at once.

"It's just something stupid I wrote." She grabbed the front of his shirt, using his chest for leverage, and jumped again. "Give it to me."

"Stupid, my ass. This is brilliant and beautiful." *Just like you.* "What are you doing working here, when you can sing like that? You should be onstage."

She tried to pull his arm down. "Stop being ridiculous and give me the phone."

He swept his arm around her waist, holding her against him as he said, "Come to Undercover tomorrow and sing for open-mic night. It's Valentine's Day. You'll make everyone's night that much more special."

She scoffed and grabbed his shirt, using his chest for leverage as she went up on her toes to try to reach the phone. "*No.* I can't sing in front of people. I just do it for myself."

He tightened his arm around her, holding her gaze. Her voice was miraculous. It was inspiring and stunning, just like her. He couldn't let this go. "How about you do it for *me*?"

Her lips parted, and she gazed at him from beneath long dark lashes. Her fingers fisted in his shirt. Sexual tension billowed as thick as the silence between them. Whether she'd sing for him or not, he knew he'd never forget the emotions he'd heard in her voice as she sang about feeling lost and found at once or the way every word sounded as though it was ripped from her soul. He wanted to be part of those emotions, to ease her longing and help her get found.

Headlights swept past the front windows, cutting through the heat. Her eyes turned apologetic, regretful even, and his gut ached.

"I have to go," she said, but her hand was fisted in his shirt.

"I need to hear you sing, sweetheart." He lowered his arm, but when he set the phone in her hand he didn't let go. "Say you'll come tomorrow night."

She swallowed hard, her eyes darting between him and the door. She unfurled her fingers from his shirt, pressing her hand firmly to his chest for a single hot second before saying, "I'll try," grabbing her things, and running for the door.

CHAPTER TWO

DANCE CLASS WAS just what Cree needed to work off her stress after doing everything she could to avoid Brock at work today. Luckily, Thursdays were Brock's busiest day, and he'd been tied up with training sessions every hour from the moment she'd arrived until the moment she'd left for the day. But that hadn't stopped him from leaving a note on the front desk that said, *Undercover. Eight o'clock. Be there or I might have to swipe your phone again.*

She'd been mortified last night when they were at the speed bag and her mouth had decided to spill her secrets before her brain could catch up and then again when her stupid earbuds came out. She'd wanted to click her heels and disappear. Brock was unlike any other man she'd ever met. He was rough and masculine, but he was also *always* a gentleman, and that was a unique combination. Most guys used sexual innuendos as conversation starters, like, *Hey, babe, you look hungry. I've got a flesh Popsicle you'll love,* or something equally retch-worthy. Even Justin, who thought he was her protector, would make quippy sexual innuendos, though she knew he didn't mean them. He was like the older brother she'd never had, and she loved him for it. But last night's brain-scrambling session was the first time Brock had ever used a sexual innuendo toward her, and just like that it had turned her mind to dust.

If Brock had cornered her at work today, she would have put her foot in her mouth again, because every time she saw him, her body vibrated with desire, remembering how incredible he'd felt pressed against her back. And oh, how she'd loved hearing those steamy innuendos coming out of his sexy mouth. Brock Garner was too all-consumingly *hot* for just dreams. The bastard had starred in her erotic fantasies. She'd imagined his perfectly manicured scruff between her thighs, her fingers fisted in his dark-blond hair as he made her come with his mouth. And his big hands covering her breasts as he took her from behind. And those eyes? Good Lord, his eyes were like sexual *beings*. They said *I'm going to fuck you hard, then love you good.* And boy did she want that and so much more.

"Great job, girls," Jana said, clapping her hands at the end of their hip-hop class, snapping Cree from her fantasies. "Y'all were hotter than Hades tonight!"

You have no idea, Cree thought as she realized her panties were damp, and not from sweat. There was probably some sin wrapped up in fantasizing about Jana's brother. She looked around to see if anyone else had noticed her zoning out during the class, but her friends Bella and Jenna were busy guzzling water. Bella and Jenna *loved* to give her advice, like older sisters. They were both married to great guys, and they had the most adorable little girls.

"Thanks for a great class," Cree said to Jana. She really liked Jana, who was tough but sweet and an incredible dancer. She used to box competitively, though she'd stopped when she got married. It was always fun when she came to the club to work out with Brock. He got all overprotective, and Jana just rolled her eyes. Cree knew all about overprotective guys. Her father was part of the Dark Knights motorcycle club in Maryland. She'd grown up around hard-core, protective bikers, which was why she didn't get too upset at Justin's overprotectiveness. She expected it. He was a member of the Cape Cod chapter of the Dark Knights.

"Thanks for coming. I'm glad you enjoyed it," Jana said. As she spoke Bella and Jenna joined them, and the other girls in the class waved on their way out the door. "You looked a little sidetracked at the end of class. Thinking about your big Valentine's Day plans?"

Oh, that? I was just mentally molesting your brother.

"I bet she's planning to take her hot biker for a *ride*." Bella waggled her blond brows.

Bella and Jenna had grown up together, and they both owned summer cottages in the Seaside community. Bella was tall and strong, with a little extra fluff around the middle, and she was the biggest prankster Cree had ever met, while Jenna was just under five feet, with curves that could make an impotent man hard. Jenna was OCD about everything from matching lingerie, socks, and earrings to alphabetizing her pantry. Cree adored them both, and she fit right in with her own quirks.

"I told you Justin and I are only friends," Cree said for the millionth time. "I grew up with his cousins, and he thinks it's his job to watch over me. That's what—"

"*The Dark Knights do*," the three of them said at the same time as Cree.

"I still think it's more than just that," Bella said.

Cree sighed. "You guys really need to stop with the Justin nonsense."

"Or maybe you should admit to the hot tryst we all hope you're enjoying," Jana said. "My brother said Justin drives you to and from work a *lot*."

"Yeah, whenever my car is on the rag." Her ancient Tercel was on its last legs. "Okay, you want to hear just how *not* into Justin I am? All of my single friends had plans for Valentine's Day, so I had to ask *Justin* to go out with me so I don't look like a loser walking into a bar alone tonight."

"Oh, that's serious *like*. It sounds a lot like me and Pete," Jenna said. "I was in love with him for *years* before we finally got together. So there's hope for you and Justin!"

"Oh my God, Jenna!" Cree swatted Jenna's arm. "Listen to me. Justin is *not* the focus of my fantasies, okay? I've been trying to catch this other guy's attention, who is *not* Justin, and I think I finally *have*. But I could use your help. I really want to turn up the heat, you know?" *And hopefully wow him enough that he'll forget about my singing.* Although she was hoping *he* might get up and sing. Until recently she'd waitressed most nights, and she'd never been able to go see him sing. She'd finally quit that job, and now she wouldn't miss seeing him sing for anything in the world. "I want to look irresistible, so I stand out among the crowd.

But my entire wardrobe is anything but sexy. Do you know where I can get something at the last minute?"

"Oh, you're sexing it up tonight? Fun!" Jana motioned in the direction of the people coming through the door and said, "I have to get ready for my last class, but here's my best sexy advice: *low cut, high heels, high hem.* It gets Hunter every time. Now, get your butts out of here so I'm not running late for my man tonight." She blew them kisses and went to greet her students.

"How long have you known this guy?" Bella asked as they put on their coats.

"A long time. He's my friend's brother." *And my other friend's brother-in-law.* "But I've only gotten to know him better over the past few months, and I really like him. The get-flustered-every-time-he's-around and lay-my-heart-on-the-table type of like. You know, the kind that makes you say shit you shouldn't?"

"I love that new-relationship feeling," Bella said on the way outside.

"Well, the feeling isn't new, and we're definitely not in a relationship, so I could be way off base. I never believed in love at first sight or anything, but I swear the first time I saw him, I was like *whoa.* He's got these perfectly plump, kissable lips, eyes that make me want to do all sorts of dirty things, and his hands. They're so big and strong, I imagine all sorts of things I probably shouldn't. When we finally talked, like, really talked, not just a passing hello when I'd see him around town, I realized he was different from other guys. He's got no pretense. No bullshit facade to work through. He's kind and funny and *so* smart and business minded. I love that about him." She could go on for hours, but she closed her mouth before she said something that could lead them back to Brock. She wanted to keep his identity to herself, just in case tonight's plan went ass over teakettle. "Anyway, I need something cute to wear."

"Yes, you do," Bella agreed. "But no place is open around here in the winter. Do you have time to go to Hyannis?"

Hyannis was forty minutes away. "*Ugh*, no. I only have about two hours to get ready, and I still have to shower and do my hair."

"Don't worry," Jenna said. "You're only a few inches taller than me, and you're boobilicious like me, so I'm sure I have something that'll fit. Can you swing by my place?"

"Great idea. I'll meet you guys there," Bella said.

"You sure you don't mind?" Cree asked. "Will it mess

up your schedule with your girls?"

"Are you kidding?" Jenna rubbed her hands together and said, "Seaside Sex-Up Girls at your service! Besides, Pete and Caden have dates with their little princesses tonight." Pete and Caden were Jenna's and Bella's husbands.

"And dates with their big princesses tomorrow night," Bella added with a wink.

Cree squealed. "Thank you! I'll go home and shower really fast, and then I'll head over."

AN HOUR LATER Cree stood in Jenna's bedroom feeling like a stuffed sausage in one of Jenna's clingy dresses. The bed was covered in dresses, skirts, and blouses. Cree had tried on six outfits already, and she felt like an imposter in every one of them. She wasn't like her sister, Isla, who worked in their parents' flower shop and loved all things girlie. But now Cree wondered if she'd just never had the right motivation to explore that side of herself, because she wanted to find the perfect mix of feminine and sexy for Brock. And what she had on felt like she was trying too hard. Even for a girl who was trying extra hard, it was a little much.

"Justin won't let me leave my house dressed like this," she said, tugging at the hemline that barely covered her ass. "I don't think I can do this. Maybe it was a stupid idea."

"Whoa, Nelly," Bella said. "You've got a body that could stop a clock, and we're not going to let you spend the rest of your life afraid to own that."

"I *own* it," she said as she sat on the edge of the bed. "I just don't *flaunt* it. These outfits are gorgeous, but they don't feel like me."

"Because they're not *yours*. Don't worry. Jenna owns more clothes than anyone I know. We'll find the right dress."

Jenna went to her closet and said, "Do you have blue heels?"

"No. Just black." She didn't love wearing heels, but she had no problem pulling up her big-girl panties and going all out tonight. Except for singing. She couldn't sing in front of anyone else. But the way Brock had said *I need to hear you sing, sweetheart. Say you'll come tomorrow night* made her want to sing for *him* and *come* for him. Heat spread up her chest, and she fanned her face, pushing to her feet and wiggling out of the dress.

Bella laughed. "What was that hot flash from?"

"You don't want to know," Cree said, and she headed into the closet. "Am I being too picky? I just want to seduce the hell out of him once and for all, so he can't stop himself from taking everything he wants."

"Then hell no, you're not being too picky," Jenna said as she whipped through dresses, which were separated by color and season. "We need to go in for the kill. *Shimmery, short,* and *sinful.*"

"Why don't you just say, 'Hey, dude. I'm totally into you. Wanna get down and dirty?'" Bella suggested.

Jenna laughed, a cackle of a sound. "Listen to you. Like *you'd* ever have said that to Caden before you were going out?"

"Hey, cut me a break. I was stuck in a window with my ass hanging out the first time he saw me. That's as good as offering myself up on a silver platter." Bella stepped into the closet with them and said, "What's that black sleeveless dress?"

"It's not shimmery," Jenna said.

"But it's sexy without being over the top. Isn't that the one with the choker?" Bella pushed past them and grabbed a hanger. She held up a black sleeveless dress. The top was fitted, but the skirt was flared. She lifted up another piece of black material and turned the dress around. "This choker is attached to the back. See? It hides the zipper."

"Wow, that's really cute!" Cree snagged the hanger.

The girls were miracle workers. Not only did Cree adore the dress, but Jenna had matching sparkly black and silver earrings and bangles. They also gave her a makeover, with smoky eyes and reddish-pink lipstick that made her look so *hot* she barely recognized herself.

An hour later Cree was walking up to the entrance of Undercover with Justin as he harassed her about looking *too* sexy, which confirmed how great she felt in the outfit. Now, if she could only get rid of the freaking butterflies swarming in her stomach.

"You'd better keep that jacket on," Justin said.

She'd worn her short leather jacket over the dress, which was nowhere near warm enough for the cold breeze sweeping up the dunes. But it went with the dress and made her feel more like herself. Besides, even though Undercover was located on a bluff overlooking the bay, it wasn't like she would be outside all night.

"No, and if you don't stop, I'm going to tear a slit in the side of this thing just to piss you off."

Justin glared at her with his ice-blue eyes as he pulled the door open. "What did you say this dude's name was?"

"I didn't," she said teasingly as they walked into the

dimly lit bar. She looped her arm through his and said, "But I *really* appreciate you coming with me. I couldn't have come on my own."

The crowded bar was decorated with sparkly red hearts hanging from the ceiling for Valentine's Day. Music played from the speakers, and on the stage were three microphones for open-mic night. A tickle of excitement skated through her as she pictured Brock onstage.

"You could have, Cree," Justin said. "You're not used to stepping out of your comfort zone, but there's nothing you *can't* do."

"See why I love you? You pester me to keep me in line, and then you build me up so I can't get too irritated with you." She embraced him and whispered, "I'm so nervous. I really like this guy."

He hugged her tighter and said, "You're gorgeous, smart, and interesting. Stop worrying and just be yourself."

"No lecture about keeping my clothes on or remembering that you can kick any guy's ass if I need you to?"

Justin smiled and said, "Sounds like you know my spiel. You're a big girl. If this guy has drawn you out of your hidey-hole, there's a reason. I'm here if you need me, but I trust your gut, so you should, too."

He hugged her again, and as he kissed her cheek, she

saw Brock walking toward the bar. Her pulse raced. She couldn't believe she was really doing this! Brock turned, his eyes sweeping over the entrance. In the next breath, those piercing blue eyes locked on her.

BROCK FELT LIKE he'd been punched in the gut. He'd been watching the door all night, hoping Cree would show up. He'd talked himself into believing she'd show up *without* Justin, that she'd felt the connection between them and it wasn't just in his head. He wanted to haul Cree out of Justin's arms and show her that she belonged with *him*, but that would make him the type of asshole he hated.

He clenched his jaw and made a beeline for the bar.

Of course she'd come with Justin. He was an idiot to hope for anything else. She'd been with him for years, and regardless of what Brock wanted, he needed to accept that it was time for him to move the hell on.

If only it were that easy.

Some women were unremarkable. Cree Redmond was *unforgettable.*

And her voice…

Sweet Jesus, her voice. He'd never heard anything like it.

Even if he couldn't be with her, he needed to hear her sing again. Hell, the *world* needed to hear her sing.

Ignoring the women eyeing him as he leaned across the bar, he flagged down Colton. He was used to women checking him out, and yeah, he could have used it to his advantage all these years and fucked anyone he wanted. But that wasn't who he was. He wanted forever love like his parents had. He wanted to be with a woman who made him as happy as she did horny. A partner in life who was funny and enlightening and could hold a conversation beyond, *Hey, let's hook up*, or *Hi, you're hot*. A woman who respected herself enough not to sleep with every guy in town. And damn it, every iota of his being told him that woman was Cree. He'd caught her reading the *The Week* magazine as often as he'd caught her surfing silly memes on Pinterest, and regardless of which one she was looking at, she'd blink those gorgeous eyes up at him and say, *A girl's gotta keep up with current events.*

"Why do you look like you want to kill someone?" Colton asked. His white-blond hair was slicked back from his face, making his chiseled features even more prominent.

"Because I'm a fucking idiot. Pour me a whiskey, will ya?"

Colton's eyes narrowed. He lowered his voice and said,

"Want to talk about it? I can get Britt to take over up here."

He was more thoughtful and less opinionated than Brock or their sisters, and they'd leaned on each other many times. But tonight wasn't going to be one of those times. "Just the whiskey, but thanks."

"If you change your mind, I'm around." Colton smirked and said, "Until I'm *not*." His gaze drifted to the other end of the bar, where a good-looking guy sat watching them.

"Excuse me. Excuse me."

Cree's voice drifted into Brock's ears, and his heart pounded like a freaking drum in his chest. She was pushing through the crowd toward the bar, smiling, her eyes trained on him, and she looked utterly *stunning*. He'd been so irritated when he'd first seen her with Justin, he hadn't noticed her makeup. She was naturally beautiful and rarely wore much makeup. But tonight her eyes were heavily lined, with a smoky shadow on her lids, and her gorgeous lips were painted, making them even more enticing. She burst through the crowd, and *holy fuck*. She looked sinful in the slinky black dress, all that creamy inked skin on display, with a black choker around her neck. She looked fuckable, lovable, and so damn pretty he was going to lose his mind.

Forget giving up on Cree.

Brock was about to become the asshole he'd swore he'd never be.

CHAPTER THREE

CREE WIGGLED BETWEEN Brock and the woman standing beside him and leaned on the bar, giving him an enticing view of her cleavage.

"Hi," she said breathily, and then she turned those devastating brown eyes on Colton. "Hey, Colton. Can I get an ice water, please?"

"Anything for you, beautiful." Colton went to get their drinks.

Brock thanked the powers that be that Colton was gay, because he'd take on anyone for his little sprite-turned-vixen, even his brother.

Cree smiled at Brock and said, "I made it, but I'm not going to sing."

"Yeah, you are," he said.

"No, I'm not. I told you I don't sing for other people."

"I bet you sing for Justin."

She scoffed. "Hardly."

"Aw, come on, sweetheart. With a voice like that, you can't tell me your boyfriend doesn't beg you to sing for him, because if you were mine, I'd want to hear it every damn day."

Colton set their drinks down, winked at Brock, and went to help another patron.

Cree stared at Brock, mouth agape, for so long, he couldn't tell if she was pissed about his comment or not. She abruptly picked up her glass and gulped a mouthful of ice water.

"You think *Justin* is my *boyfriend?*"

He raised his brow, unsure why that would come as a surprise to her.

She laughed and shook her head. "Seriously? What is it with people around here? He's like a brother to me and definitely *not* my boyfriend."

Relief and desire rushed through Brock like a gale-force wind. He downed his drink in one swig, his mind sprinting around that little golden nugget, needing to be sure he'd heard her correctly. "But he drives you to and from work all the time."

"Yeah, because my car sucks and I can't ride my bike when it's too cold or rainy. Do you really think I'd be flirting with you all the time if I had a boyfriend? That is so *not* me."

"I just assumed…"

Her eyes widened. "You thought he drove me because we were sleeping together? *Ohmygosh!* All this time?"

"All this time." He stepped closer, no longer having a reason to keep his distance. Their bodies brushed, and he fucking loved the way her breathing hitched. "So you haven't been *with* Justin?"

"No," she said a little breathlessly. "We're close, but not like that."

He belted his arm around her waist, hauling her against him. His whole body ached for her as her lips parted and her tongue swept over them. He threaded his hand into her hair, twining the silky locks around his fingers as he searched her eyes and found the green light he was looking for.

"I'm your boss, so if this feels wrong"—he brushed his lips over hers—"you're *fired.*"

He slanted his mouth over hers, crushing their bodies together. Her soft curves melded to his hard frame. She clung to him, meeting every stroke of his tongue with an eager one of her own, filling his lungs with her sexy moans. That titillating vibration unleashed all of his pent-up desires. He tugged her hair, angling her mouth so he could deepen the kiss. Her hands dove into his hair like she'd been waiting her whole life for this moment, and he loved it. Kissing Cree was everything he'd imagined and more. She was passionate, seductive, and hungry for *him*. But somewhere in the recesses of his mind voices filtered in, and he remembered they were at the bar, surrounded by strangers. The urge to protect her with everything he had surged forth, forcing him to ease his efforts. He kissed her tenderly, not wanting to stop but knowing he had to.

He loved the sweet sounds of surrender she made and the whimpers that fell from her lips as he finally forced himself to reluctantly draw back.

Her cheeks were flushed, her lipstick kissed off, and she was even more gorgeous than ever because she was *finally* in his arms.

She whispered, "Kiss me again," like a secret.

He took her in a slow, sensual kiss, leaving her breathless.

Keeping her close, he pressed a kiss beside her ear and said, "I'm going to *devour* you." He slicked his tongue around the shell of her ear. "And then I'm going to fuck you."

She shuddered against him, her fingers digging into the back of his neck.

"And just when you think I'm done, I'm going to make love to you so thoroughly, you won't remember what your body felt like without me in it."

"Yes," she pleaded in a rush of warm breath.

He took her chin between his finger and thumb, gazing deeply into her eyes as he said, "Right after you get up on that stage and sing for me."

CREE HAD NO idea how her noodle legs were carrying her as Brock led her through the crowd. Didn't he know she was still trying to catch her breath? He'd shattered her ability to think the second his mouth had touched hers, and those kisses? *Lethal.* She needed to change her panties! He didn't just kiss; he consumed, *possessed.* How had he known she'd love him tugging her hair or kissing her so deeply she couldn't tell where she ended and he began? Heat spiked down her spine with the memory. She was going to lose her mind before the night was over. She was sure of it. He'd freed *years* of longing. Her body was pulsing with it, and on top of it all, he wanted her to do the unthinkable? To sing in front of all these people? She *couldn't* do it. But with Brock's sexy promises hanging like gleaming brass rings, she wanted to try.

"Hey, man," Brock said, jerking Cree from her thoughts and bringing Justin and his brothers sitting at a table into focus. "I just wanted to let you know Cree's in good hands tonight. I'll make sure she gets home safely."

Justin looked from Brock to Cree, and she felt herself grinning like a fool as he rose to his feet and asked, for her ears only, "Babe, you good?"

"Mm-hm. Yes. Definitely. Better than good." Could she ramble *more*?

Justin's eyes drifted from her to Brock and back again. "Why didn't you just tell me it was Brock? He's a good guy."

"Because if he wasn't into me, I'd have looked like a fool," she said softly.

Apparently not soft enough, because Brock pulled her closer and said, "Sweetheart, any man who isn't into you is a fool. But now they'll have to go through me."

He slipped a finger beneath her chin, tipped her face up to his, and kissed her, right there in front of everyone. He was claiming her, and she'd wanted this for so long, it made her a little giddy. Even that simple press of his delicious lips made her swoon.

They left Justin and made their way to another table,

where Sawyer and Sky were sitting. Sky squinted, confusion rising in her eyes as Brock pulled out a chair for Cree. They sat down, and Brock's arm circled her shoulders.

"Um…?" Sky flipped her long dark hair over her shoulder. "What is *this*?"

Sawyer arched a brow at Brock.

"Turns out Cree's not seeing Justin after all," Brock said.

"You thought she was seeing *Justin*?" Sky asked.

Cree hiked a thumb at Brock. "Along with Bella, Jenna, and God knows who else."

"Wow. If I'd known you were into Cree, I could have clued you into the fact that she's been jonesing for you forever!"

Brock's brows slanted, and he glowered at Sawyer. "You couldn't tell me that?"

Sawyer splayed his hands. "Dude, this is the first I'm hearing of it."

Cree and Sky shared a laugh.

"I swore her to secrecy," Cree confessed, happiness and heat still pulsing inside her. "Bad move on my part, huh?"

"I'd say." Brock pulled her in for another scorching kiss. "That just means we have a lot of time to make up for."

"Geez, Brock. Why do you think she applied for a job at a boxing club? Because she *loves* boxing?" Sky rolled her eyes.

Brock squeezed Cree's shoulder with a look of disbelief. "Is that true?"

"Yes, but I love my job. I get to see you every day and watch you work out, shirtless and sweaty, and..." She fanned her face. "I need ice water."

Everyone laughed.

"But there is one thing," Cree said.

Brock gazed into her eyes like she was all he ever wanted and said, "Anything."

"Does this mean I can stop learning to box? I did it to get closer to you, but my arms are so sore after we work out. I want to learn to protect myself, but..." She rubbed her biceps.

He laughed and kissed her again, making her wish she had a hundred more questions just to earn more of his kisses. "I think we can find more enjoyable ways to work out together. And I can show you other self-defense moves."

"*What* is going on over here?" Jana asked as she and Hunter joined them. "You didn't tell me we were sexing you up for my *brother*!"

Cree winced. "Sorry."

"Oh, heck no. Don't be sorry." Jana whipped out her phone and said, "I'm assuming the goofy look on Brock's face means you two *are* together, right? I mean, this will probably be more than a one-night stand?"

God, I hope so.

"Definitely," Brock said.

"Then I just won a hundred bucks! At our wedding I bet Harper you two would end up together. I have to text her," Jana said as she typed out a text. Their sister Harper was a screenplay writer and was currently out of town working on her first optioned script.

"That was a *long* time ago," Cree said, eyeing Brock. Could he have possibly liked her as long as she'd liked him? Brock squeezed her hand, nodding with so much honesty in his eyes, she melted inside.

Jana set her phone down and said, "When I saw how Brock looked at you, it was so different from the way he'd ever looked at any other woman, and I just knew." She smiled at Hunter and said, "I told you so."

"I thought you and Justin were an item," Hunter explained. Then he kissed Jana and said, "*And* my wife likes to gloat."

Jana swatted him and climbed into his lap the way Cree

hoped one day she could climb into Brock's.

"Hey, you know that Maroon 5 song 'Love Somebody'?" Brock asked out of the blue.

"Doesn't everyone?" Sky said.

"I belt it out when I'm home alone and it comes on my playlist," Cree said.

"Where are my A Capella Boys?" Roach's voice boomed from a microphone. He was a mountain of muscle, like Brock, with jet-black hair and serious eyes.

Cheers and applause rang out.

"That's us, sweetheart." Brock rose to his feet, bringing Cree up beside him.

"*Us?*" She looked at Sawyer, who shrugged.

"That's right," Brock said as he led her toward the stage.

"Brock? I told you I can't sing in front of people." She felt dizzy and sick as he dragged her up the steps. "Brock!" she whispered harshly. "I can't do this. *Please!*"

He spun her into his arms, captivating her with a heated stare, which was totally unfair. "Do you trust me?"

"Yes, but—" Her words were lost on the press of his lips. His arms circled her, and she was vaguely aware of hoots and cheers increasing as they kissed.

She couldn't walk off the stage now if she wanted to.

Her legs were like Jell-O.

"I've got you, sweetheart," he said with a smile. "Hopefully that helped you relax."

"Are you nuts? I'm more wound up than ever," she confessed, her cheeks burning.

"Damn. Sorry about that." The glimmer in his eyes told her he was *sort of* sorry. "But please don't keep that gorgeous voice all to yourself. It's too special not to be given a stage of its own." He stood in front of her, blocking her view of the cheering audience. "Focus on me and only me."

Her heart slammed against her ribs, and she felt like she might pass out, but she wasn't sure if it was from nerves or from his kisses. He was looking at her like he not only adored her, but as if her singing meant the world to him. And that made her want to try.

He grabbed a microphone and put it in her shaking hands. Then Colton crossed the stage and handed a microphone to Brock. Colton winked at Cree as he headed off the stage.

Brock stared directly into her eyes, his back to the audience even as he spoke into the microphone and said, "There's been a slight change to the A Capella Boys. Joining the A Capella Boys tonight is the beautiful *bella*

Cree Redmond."

More cheers rang out, and her pulse skyrocketed. Brock's deep voice filled the air as he said, "Remember her name, ladies and gentlemen, because this talented lady is going to be *big*."

Her heart nearly climbed out of her chest.

He nodded at Roach and Sawyer, and then he pinned her in place with a stare that held as much confidence as hope. The three men began moving to a nonexistent beat as they sang about pills that were hard to swallow and being unable to recover if they fell for someone. Cree focused on Brock's eyes as they gazed deeply into hers and on his lips as he sang the chorus. It seemed like every word was meant for her as he sang about their only being halfway there and wanting to go all the way. He hadn't written the words, but he didn't have to. He still drove each one into her heart, coaxing her along with his rich, deep voice and hungry eyes, drowning out her inhibitions as he sang about wanting her to stay with him tonight.

Her voice came softly at first. She sang about being unable to recover if *she* fell for *him* and how she thought about *him* every day. The lyrics rang so true, she realized she was singing from her heart, asking him not to leave her tonight and to stay with her tomorrow. Adrenaline rushed through her, sending her words soaring with such vehemence, she found herself dancing with Brock as the truth poured out, without a care of who else heard her as long as he did. She *was* a bit lost. She had *no* idea where to start with him, but she felt herself falling even harder, and she never wanted to stop.

The crowd went wild, and she realized Roach and Sawyer were no longer on the stage. Brock's soulful eyes drilled into her as he sang the chorus, and her mind traveled to the strangest place, to a tattoo she'd gotten shortly before she'd met him. It was a single line from a poem she'd found scrawled on a napkin at a bar where she'd worked. She'd never known what had compelled her to have *In your eyes I found myself* inked on her skin until tonight. Now it all made sense.

After he sang the last note, the room exploded around them. Brock swept her into his arms, taking her in a kiss that seared through her like lightning, causing another burst of applause and cheers.

She laughed into their kisses, tears stinging her eyes. Never had she felt so alive, so invigorated, or so lost in a single person. "That was amazing! Thank you!"

"You're amazing, Cree, and I'm going to make sure you know it every single day from here on out."

"Starting with making good on every one of your naughty promises, I hope."

A SHORT WHILE later they stumbled into Brock's Wellfleet cottage, tearing at each other's clothing, leaving a trail from his front door to the bedroom. Moonlight streamed in through the open curtains as he backed her up against the wall, his thick cock pressing into her belly. His hands moved over her flesh roughly as they feasted on each other's mouths. He bit her lower lip enticingly, tugging gently, his eyes a torrent of greed and lust.

"I've waited so long for you," he rasped.

"I'm yours, Brock," she panted out, and she meant it. She'd been with two men in her life, and both encounters had taken place long before she'd first seen Brock.

"You look gorgeous tonight," he said between ravenous kisses. "But for the record, I think you're sinfully hot in anything you wear. And I really dig your boots."

She smiled against his lips. "You do?"

"Hell yes. Your boots, your yoga pants, those T-shirts you wear." He kissed her deeply and said, "I'm clean, sweetheart. Please tell me you're on birth control."

"I am."

"Thank Christ," he growled, taking her in another scorching kiss. "I want to feel your heat surrounding me when I'm buried deep inside you."

"Yes" came out as a breathless plea as he kissed, bit, and sucked his way down her body.

He slowed to love her breasts, squeezing one nipple between his finger and thumb as he drove her out of her mind sucking and teasing the other. When his teeth scraped her sensitive skin, she bowed off the wall with the spikes of pleasure and pain it sent to her core.

"Oh, *yes!*" she cried out, and he did it again.

She cupped his balls, earning a guttural moan so *hot* she got goose bumps. She wanted to drop to her knees and take his thick cock in her mouth, but he was on the move, his talented mouth loving its way south. He slicked his tongue over each of her tattoos, and when he reached her belly button, he took the ring between his teeth and tugged. Then he plunged his tongue into her belly button. He clutched her ass, lavishing her belly with licks and sucks and openmouthed kisses. She swore she felt every one of them between her legs.

She bit her lower lip as he continued blazing a path to the apex of her thighs.

"Open your eyes, gorgeous," he said, as much a demand as a request. When she met his gaze, he said, "I want to see your face when you come on my mouth."

Her sex clenched in anticipation. In the next second, he dragged his tongue between her wet, swollen lips, sending sparks skating along her skin, and her head fell back with a greedy moan.

"Watch me, sweetheart," he said more demandingly.

And she did.

Holy heck…

His tongue and hands were wicked, licking and sucking, plunging and teasing, until she was a thrusting, begging mess of raw nerves. When he used his tongue on her clit and dipped his fingers inside her, finding that magical spot with the precision of a heat-seeking missile, she cried out, tugging at his hair and holding his stare. The pleasure in his eyes intensified hers, and she came that much harder.

When she collapsed limply against the wall, she pulled him up by his hair, and he crushed his mouth to hers. He tasted of her, but she didn't care. She'd never experienced anything as potent as this incredible man, and she wanted to give him the same blissful feelings he gave her.

She splayed her hand on his chest, putting space between them as she slid down the wall to her knees, eye to eye with his beautiful cock.

"Sweetheart, tonight is supposed to be about you," he said, running his thick fingers through her hair.

She grinned seductively up at him. "It *is*."

Licking him from base to tip, she watched him watching her as his fingers fisted in her hair. She licked him again, and his chin dropped with a sharp exhalation. She lowered her mouth over his cock, working him with her hand and mouth, sucking and squeezing. The noises he made, the tension in his thighs, emboldened her, and she quickened her efforts, hoping he'd really let go.

He groaned, and she felt his tension mounting and knew he was struggling to keep himself in check.

She drew back and said, "Fuck my mouth, but don't come." She had no idea if it was even possible for him to give her all he had without coming, but she wanted to find out. She wanted to do *everything* with him, test every boundary, give herself wholly over to them.

"I will, sweetheart, but first I need to kiss that sexy mouth of yours." He hauled her up to her feet, claiming her in another penetrating kiss. His tongue plunged savagely into her mouth as his hand dove between her legs, expertly taking her up to the edge and catapulting her toward the stars. He continued kissing her through the very last pulse of her orgasm, and when he drew back and gazed into her eyes, she wondered what he saw.

"I didn't want to just love somebody," he said roughly, and she realized he was referring to the lyrics they'd sang. "I want you, Cree, only you."

That made her feel all kinds of terrific. "Me too."

This time she *slinked* down his body, unhurried, kissing his pecs, sucking his nipples, pressing her lips, and slicking her tongue all over his abs. When she finally lowered her mouth over his shaft, he made a purely masculine sound. His hands pushed into her hair, and she grabbed his ass, pulling him forward, giving him the okay to do as she'd asked.

And he did.

Gloriously.

He panted out his appreciation. "So good…Want more of you…*Fuuck…Oh yeah, right there. Like that…*"

When she felt him swell inconceivably bigger in her hand, she released him, slowly dragging her tongue around the broad head of his cock. But she barely had time to catch her breath before he lifted her off her feet and lowered her onto his hard length. She felt every inch of him. She couldn't stifle her astonished, *elated* sounds. He filled her so completely, so perfectly, she felt lighter, sexier, and more complete at once.

He lowered them to the bed without breaking their connection, and a perplexed expression came over his handsome face. "*God*, Cree. Do you feel that? It's like the world just shifted."

She nodded, for fear of choking up if she spoke.

"I want to discover *everything* about you, *with* you, about *us*. Every pleasure point, every pet peeve." He kissed her deeply. "I want to fulfill my every promise, but before I fuck you, I need to make love to you and savor every single second of being close to you."

Tears stung her eyes, and worry rose in his.

"No lovemaking?"

"No, I mean, *yes*," she said shakily. "I want that, too. I want everything with you."

His mouth descended on hers, and he loved her slowly, sensually, and as promised, he loved her thoroughly.

A LONG WHILE later, they lay spent on the mattress, their bodies tangled together. Cree couldn't remember ever feeling happier and more at peace.

"Happy Valentine's Day, beautiful," he said, kissing her softly.

"Best Valentine's Day *ever*."

He shifted his big body over her and laced their fingers together with a devilish look in his eyes. "Wait until you see what I have in store for Fridays." He nipped at her jaw.

"Fridays?"

"Why limit our celebrations to holidays? Tempt-You Thursdays." He kissed her neck. "Fuck-Me Fridays. Suck-Me Saturdays." He kissed her lips. "Savor-You Sundays."

She rocked against him, and like a gift from the heavens above, he got hard again.

"If you survive," he said coyly, "maybe we'll make it to Marry-Me Monday…"

She laughed, but her heart swelled to near bursting even as she said, "Let's not get too far ahead of ourselves."

"Says the girl who once refused to sing for me."

He silenced her with a sinfully delicious kiss, and as their bodies came together, she had a feeling she'd never be able to deny him a damn thing.

Ready for more fun, sexy Seaside love stories?

If this was your first introduction to Seaside Summers, turn the page for a preview of Bella and Caden's story, SEASIDE DREAMS, the first book in the Seaside Summers series. The love stories of Jenna and Pete, Sky and Sawyer, Jana and Hunter, and many more Seaside friends are also available for your binge-reading pleasure.

Bella Abbascia has returned to Seaside Cottages in Wellfleet, Massachusetts, as she does every summer. Only this year, Bella has more on her mind than sunbathing and skinny-dipping with her girlfriends. She's quit her job, put her house on the market, and sworn off relationships while she builds a new life in her favorite place on earth. That is, until good-time Bella's prank takes a bad turn and a sinfully sexy police officer appears on the scene.

Single father and police officer Caden Grant left Boston with his fourteen-year-old son, Evan, after his partner was killed in the line of duty. He hopes to find a safer life in the small resort town of Wellfleet, and when he meets Bella during a night patrol shift, he realizes he's found the one thing he'd never allowed himself to hope for—or even realized he was missing.

After fourteen years of focusing solely on his son, Caden cannot resist the intense attraction he feels toward beautiful Bella, and Bella's powerless to fight the heat of their budding romance. But starting over proves more difficult than either of them imagined, and when Evan gets mixed up with the wrong kids, Caden's loyalty is put to the test. Will he give up everything to protect his son—even Bella?

CHAPTER ONE

BELLA ABBASCIA STRUGGLED to keep her grip on a ceramic toilet as she crossed the gravel road in Seaside, the community where she spent her summers. It was one o'clock in the morning, and Bella had a prank in store for Theresa Ottoline, a straitlaced Seaside resident and the elected property manager for the community. Bella and two of her besties, Amy Maples and Jenna Ward, had polished off two bottles of Middle Sister wine while they waited for the other cottage owners to turn in for the night. Now, dressed in their nighties and a bit tipsy, they struggled to keep their grip on a toilet that Bella had spent two days painting bright blue, planting flowers in, and adorning with seashells. They were carrying the toilet to Theresa's driveway to break rule number fourteen of the Community Homeowners Association's Guidelines: *No tacky displays allowed in the front of the cottages.*

"You're sure she's asleep?" Bella asked as they came to

the grass in front of the cottage of their fourth bestie, Leanna Bray.

"Yes. She turned off her lights at eleven. We should have hidden it someplace other than my backyard. It's so far. Can we stop for a minute? This sucker is heavy." Amy drew her thinly manicured brows together.

"Oh, come on. Really? We only have a little ways to go." Bella nodded toward Theresa's driveway, which was across the road from her cottage, about a hundred feet away.

Amy glanced at Jenna for support. Jenna nodded, and the two lowered their end to the ground, causing Bella to nearly drop hers.

"That's so much better." Jenna tucked her stick-straight brown hair behind her ear and shook her arms out to her sides. "Not all of us lift weights for breakfast."

"Oh, please. The most exercise I get during the summer is lifting a bottle of wine," Bella said. "Carrying around those boobs of yours is more of a workout."

Jenna was just under five feet tall with breasts the size of bowling balls and a tiny waist. She could have been the model for the modern-day Barbie doll, while Bella's figure was more typical for an almost thirty-year-old woman. Although she was tall, strong, and relatively lean, she refused to give up her comfort foods, which left her a little soft in places, with a figure similar to Julia Roberts or Jennifer Lawrence.

"I don't carry them with my arms." Jenna looked down at her chest and cupped a breast in each hand. "But yeah, that would be great exercise."

Amy rolled her eyes. Pin-thin and nearly flat chested, Amy was the most modest of the group, and in her long T-shirt and underwear, she looked like a teenager next to curvy Jenna. "We only need a sec, Bella."

They turned at the sound of a passionate moan coming from Leanna's cottage.

"She forgot to close the window again," Jenna whispered as she tiptoed around the side of Leanna's cottage. "Typical Leanna. I'm just going to close it."

Leanna had fallen in love with bestselling author Kurt Remington the previous summer, and although they had a house on the bay, they often stayed in the two-bedroom cottage so Leanna could enjoy her summer friends. The Seaside cottages in Wellfleet, Massachusetts, had been in the girls' families for years, and they had spent summers together since they were kids.

"Wait, Jenna. Let's get the toilet to Theresa's first." Bella placed her hands on her hips so they knew she meant business. Jenna stopped before she reached for the window, and Bella realized it would have been a futile effort anyway. Jenna would need a stepstool to pull that window down.

"Oh…Kurt." Leanna's voice split the night air.

Amy covered her mouth to stifle a laugh. "Fine, but let's hurry. Poor Leanna will be mortified to find out she left the window open again."

"I'm the last one who wants to hear her having sex. I'm done with men, or at least with commitments, until my life is back on track." Ever since last summer, when Leanna had met Kurt, started her own jam-making business, and moved to the Cape full-time, Bella had been thinking of making a change of her own. Leanna's success had inspired her to finally go for it. Well, that and the fact that she'd made the mistake of dating a fellow teacher, Jay Cook. It had been months since they broke up, but they'd taught at the same Connecticut high school, and until she left for the summer, she couldn't avoid running in to him on a daily basis. It was just the nudge she needed to take the plunge and finally quit her job and start over. *New job, new life, new location.* She just hadn't told her friends yet. She'd thought she would tell them the minute she arrived at Seaside and they were all together, maybe over a bottle of wine or on the beach. But Leanna had been spending a lot of time with Kurt, and every time it was just the four of them, she hadn't been ready to come clean. She knew they'd worry and ask questions, and she wanted to have some of the transition sorted out before answering them.

"Bella, you can't give up on men. Jay was just a jerk." Amy touched her arm.

She really needed to fill them in on the whole Jay and quitting her job thing. She was beyond over Jay, but they knew Bella to be the stable one of the group, and learning of her sudden change was a conversation that needed to be handled when they weren't wrestling a fifty-pound toilet.

"Fine. You're right. But I'm going to make all of my future decisions separate from any man. So…until my life is in order, no commitments for me."

"Not me. I'd give anything to have what Kurt and Leanna have," Amy said.

Bella lifted her end of the toilet easily as Jenna and Amy struggled to lift theirs. "Got it?"

"Yeah. Go quick. This damn thing is heavy," Jenna said as they shuffled along the grass.

"More…" Leanna pleaded.

Amy stumbled and lost her grip. The toilet dropped to the ground, and Jenna yelped.

"Shh. You're going to wake up the whole complex!"

Bella stalked over to them.

"Oh, Kurt!" Jenna rocked her hips. "More, baby, more!"

"Really?" Bella tried to keep a straight face, but when Leanna cried out again, she doubled over with laughter.

Amy, always the voice of reason, whispered, "Come on. We *need* to close her window."

"Yes!" Leanna cried.

They fell against one another in a fit of laughter, stumbling beside Leanna's cottage.

"I could make popcorn," Jenna said, struggling to keep a straight face.

Amy scowled at her. "She got pissed the last time you did that." She grabbed Bella's hand and whispered through gritted teeth, "Take out the screen so you can shut the window, please."

"I told you we should have put a lock on the outside of her window," Jenna reminded them. Last summer, when Leanna and Kurt had first begun dating, they'd often forgotten to close the window. To save Leanna embarrassment, Jenna had offered to be on sex-noise mission control and close the window if Leanna ever forgot to. A few drinks later, she'd mistakenly abandoned the idea for the summer.

"While you close the window, I'll get the sign for the toilet." Amy hurried back toward Bella's deck in her boy-shorts underwear and a T-shirt.

Bella tossed the screen to the side so she could reach inside and close the window. The side of Leanna's cottage was on a slight incline, and although Bella was tall, she needed to stand on her tiptoes to get a good grip on the window. The hem of the nightie caught on her underwear, exposing her ample derriere.

"Cute satin skivvies." Jenna reached out to tug Bella's shirt down and Bella swatted her.

Bella pushed as hard as she could on the top of the window, trying to ignore the sensuous moans and the creaking of bedsprings coming from inside the cottage.

"The darn thing's stuck," she whispered.

Jenna moved beside her and reached for the window. Her fingertips barely grazed the bottom edge.

Amy ran toward them, waving a long stick with a paper sign taped to the top that read, WELCOME BACK.

Leanna moaned, and Jenna laughed and lost her footing. Bella reached for her, and the window slammed shut, catching Bella's hair. Leanna's dog, Pepper, barked, sending Amy and Jenna into more fits of laughter.

With her hair caught in the window and her head plastered to the sill, Bella put a finger to her lips. "Shh!"

Headlights flashed across Leanna's cottage as a car turned up the gravel road.

"Shit!" Bella went up on her toes, struggled to lift the window and free her hair, which felt like it was being ripped from her skull. The curtains flew open and Leanna peered through the glass. Bella lifted a hand and waved. *Crap.* She heard Leanna's front door open, and Pepper bolted around the corner, barking a blue streak and knocking Jenna to the ground just as a police car rolled up next to them and shined a spotlight on Bella's ass.

CADEN GRANT HAD been with the Wellfleet Police Department for only three months, having moved after his partner of nine years was killed in the line of duty. He'd relocated to the small town with his teenage son, Evan, in hopes of working in a safer location. So far, he'd found the people of Wellfleet to be respectful and thankful for the efforts of the local law enforcement officers, a welcome change after dealing with rebellion on every corner in Boston. Wellfleet had recently experienced a rash of small thefts—cars being broken into, cottages being ransacked, and the police had begun patrolling the private communities along Route 6, communities that in the past had taken care of their own security. Caden rolled up the gravel road in the Seaside community and spotted a dog running circles around a person rolling on the ground.

He flicked on the spotlight as he rolled to a stop. *Holy Christ. What is going on?* He quickly assessed the situation. A blond woman was banging on a window with both hands. Her shirt was bunched at her waist, and a pair of black satin panties barely covered the most magnificent ass he'd seen in a long time.

"Open the effing window!" she hollered.

Caden stepped from the car. "What's going on here?" He walked around the dark-haired woman, who was rolling from side to side on the ground while laughing hysterically, and the fluffy white dog, who was barking as though his life depended on it, and he quickly realized that the blond woman's hair was caught in the window. Behind him another blonde crouched on the ground, laughing so hard she kept snorting. *Why the hell aren't any of you wearing pants?*

"Leanna! I'm stuck!" the blonde by the window yelled.

"Officer, we're sorry." The blonde behind him rose to her feet, tugging her shirt down to cover her underwear;

then she covered her mouth with her hand as more laughter escaped. The dog barked and clawed at Caden's shoes.

"Someone want to tell me what's going on here?" Caden didn't even want to try to guess.

"We're..." The brunette laughed again as she rose to her knees and tried to straighten her camisole, which barely contained her enormous breasts. She ran her eyes down Caden's body. "Well, *hello* there, handsome." She fell backward, laughing again.

Christ. Just what he needed, three drunk women.

The brunette inside the cottage lifted the window, freeing the blonde's hair, which sent her stumbling backward and crashing into his chest. There was no ignoring the feel of her seductive curves beneath the thin layer of fabric. Her hair was a thick, tangled mess. She looked up at him with eyes the color of rich cocoa and lips sweet enough to taste. The air around them pulsed with heat. Christ, she was beautiful.

"Whoa. You okay?" he asked. He told his arms to let her go, but there was a disconnect, and his hands remained stuck to her waist.

"It's...It's not what it looks like." She dropped her eyes to her hands, clutching his forearms, and she released him fast, as if she'd been burned. She took a step back and helped the brunette to her feet. "We were…"

"They were trying to close our window, Officer." A tall, dark-haired man came around the side of the cottage, wearing a pair of jeans and no shirt. "Kurt Remington." He held a hand out in greeting and shook his head at the women, now holding on to each other, giggling and whispering.

"Officer Caden Grant." He shook Kurt's hand. "We've had some trouble with break-ins lately. Do you know these women?" His eyes swept over the tall blonde. He followed the curve of her thighs to where they disappeared beneath her nightshirt, then drifted up to her full breasts, finally coming to rest on her beautiful dark eyes. It had been a damn long time since he'd been this attracted to a woman.

"Of course he knows us." The hot blonde stepped forward, arms crossed, eyes no longer wide and warm, but narrow and angry.

He hated men who leered at women, but he was powerless to refrain from drinking her in for one last second. The other two women were lovely in their own right, but they didn't compare to the tall blonde with fire in her eyes and a body made for loving.

Kurt nodded. "Yes, Officer. We know them."

"God, you guys. What the heck?" the dark-haired woman asked through the open window.

"You were waking the dead," the tall blonde answered.

"Oh, gosh. I'm sorry, Officer," the brunette said through the window. Her cheeks flushed, and she slipped back inside and closed the window.

"I assure you, everything is okay here." Kurt glared at the hot blonde.

"Okay, well, if you see any suspicious activity, we're only a phone call away." He took a step toward his car.

The tall blonde hurried into his path. "Did someone from Seaside call the police?"

"No. I was just patrolling the area."

She held his gaze. "Just patrolling the area? No one *patrols* Seaside."

"Bella," the other blonde hissed.

Bella.

"Seriously. No one patrols our community. They never have." She lifted her chin in a way that he assumed was meant as a challenge, but it had the opposite effect. She looked cuter than hell.

Caden stepped closer and tried to keep a straight face. "Your name is Bella?"

"Maybe."

Feisty, too. He liked that. "Well, Maybe Bella, you're right. We haven't patrolled your community in the past, but things have changed. We'll be patrolling more often to keep you safe until we catch the people who have been burglarizing the area." He leaned in close and whispered, "But you might consider wearing pants for your window-closing evening strolls. Never know who's traipsing around out here."

To continue reading, please *buy SEASIDE DREAMS

*This title is free at the time of this publication in digital format.
Price subject to change without notice.

MORE BOOKS BY MELISSA FOSTER

LOVE IN BLOOM BIG-FAMILY ROMANCE COLLECTION

SNOW SISTERS
Sisters in Love
Sisters in Bloom
Sisters in White

THE BRADENS at Weston
Lovers at Heart, Reimagined
Destined for Love
Friendship on Fire
Sea of Love
Bursting with Love
Hearts at Play

THE BRADENS at Trusty
Taken by Love
Fated for Love
Romancing My Love
Flirting with Love
Dreaming of Love
Crashing into Love

THE BRADENS at Peaceful Harbor
Healed by Love
Surrender My Love
River of Love
Crushing on Love
Whisper of Love
Thrill of Love

**THE BRADENS & MONTGOMERYS at Pleasant Hill –
Oak Falls**
Embracing Her Heart
Anything for Love

Trails of Love
Wild Crazy Hearts
Making You Mine
Searching for Love
Hot for Love
Sweet Sexy Heart
Then Came Love
Rocked by Love
Falling for Mr. Bad

THE BRADENS at Ridgeport
Playing Mr. Perfect
Sincerely, Mr. Braden

THE BRADEN NOVELLAS
Promise My Love
Our New Love
Daring Her Love
Story of Love
Love at Last
A Very Braden Christmas

THE REMINGTONS
Game of Love
Stroke of Love
Flames of Love
Slope of Love
Read, Write, Love
Touched by Love

THE RYDERS
Seized by Love
Claimed by Love
Chased by Love
Rescued by Love
Swept Into Love

SEASIDE SUMMERS

Seaside Dreams
Seaside Hearts
Seaside Sunsets
Seaside Secrets
Seaside Nights
Seaside Embrace
Seaside Lovers
Seaside Whispers
Seaside Serenade

BAYSIDE SUMMERS
Bayside Desires
Bayside Passions
Bayside Heat
Bayside Escape
Bayside Romance
Bayside Fantasies

THE STEELES AT SILVER ISLAND
Tempted by Love
My True Love
Caught by Love
Always Her Love
Wild Island Love
Enticing Her Love

THE SILVERS AT SILVER ISLAND
Flirting with Trouble
The Trouble with Flings

THE WHISKEYS: DARK KNIGHTS AT PEACEFUL HARBOR
Tru Blue
Truly, Madly, Whiskey
Driving Whiskey Wild
Wicked Whiskey Love
Mad About Moon
Taming My Whiskey

The Gritty Truth
In for a Penny
Running on Diesel

THE WHISKEYS: DARK KNIGHTS AT REDEMPTION RANCH
The Trouble with Whiskey
Freeing Sully (Prequel to For the Love of Whiskey)
For the Love of Whiskey
A Taste of Whiskey
Love, Lies, and Whiskey
My Whiskey Redemption

THE WICKEDS: DARK KNIGHTS AT BAYSIDE
A Little Bit Wicked
The Wicked Aftermath
Crazy, Wicked Love
The Wicked Truth
His Wicked Ways
Talk Wicked to Me
Irresistibly Wicked

WILD BOYS AFTER DARK
Logan
Heath
Jackson
Cooper

BAD BOYS AFTER DARK
Mick
Dylan
Carson
Brett

SUGAR LAKE
The Real Thing
Only for You
Love Like Ours

Finding My Girl (Graphic Companion Booklet)

HARMONY POINTE
Call Her Mine
This is Love
She Loves Me

SILVER HARBOR
Maybe We Will
Maybe We Should
Maybe We Won't

STANDALONE ROMANTIC COMEDIES
Hot Mess Summer
The Mr. Right Checklist

HARBORSIDE NIGHTS SERIES
Includes characters from the Love in Bloom series
Catching Cassidy
Discovering Delilah (F/F)
Tempting Tristan (M/M)

More Books by Melissa
Chasing Amanda (mystery/suspense)
Come Back to Me (mystery/suspense)
Have No Shame (historical fiction/romance)
Love, Lies & Mystery (3-book bundle)
Megan's Way (literary fiction)
Traces of Kara (psychological thriller)
Where Petals Fall (suspense)

www.MelissaFoster.com

Melissa Foster is the *New York Times, Wall Street Journal,* and *USA Today* bestselling and award-winning author of more than 100 novels. Her books have been recommended by *USA Today*'s book blog, *Hagerstown* magazine, *The Patriot,* and several other print venues.

Melissa enjoys discussing her books with book clubs and reader groups and welcomes an invitation to your event. Melissa's books are available through most online retailers in paperback, digital, and audio formats.

Melissa also writes sweet romance under the pen name Addison Cole.

9 781948 868396